Rosa

To order additional copies, please contact us.
BookSurge, LLC
www.booksurge.com
1-866-308-6235
orders@booksurge.com

To contact the author, or for
audiobooks - email: RosaItalianTale@aol.com.
Or write:
E. Ghilarducci, PO Box 738,
Calistoga, CA 94515.

EILEEN
GHILARDUCCI ARNOFF

ROSA

AN ITALIAN TALE

2005

Rosa

TABLE OF CONTENTS

Benvenuti 3
The Graziano Sisters 5
Home 7
Gramma and Grampa 9
Gramma Silent, but Furba 15
The Storyteller. 17
L'Americano. 19
Home Luxuries 21
Gramma's Job and "Lo Sciopero" 23
At The Picnic 25
Baby Brother. 29
Baby Sister. 31
Genny and Benny 33
Life with the Graziano Sisters 37
The Working Man. 39
Pa 41
The Hallway 45
Mariucce 47
Giovanni 51
The Don and Giovanni 53
The Courtship 57
Grand Avenue, Hubbard Street. 61
Cover Girl 64
Louis. 71
The Feasts 73

The Black Hand 77

Education 79

Career Path 83

Women's Lib 85

Brooks. 87

Off to War. 91

Lucky in Love 95

Asking for her Hand 97

Wedding "La Sposa". 99

The Happiest Day of My Life 103

Italian Tradition. 107

Taking Sides 111

Brooks Grocery 113

Learning the Trade. 115

The Store—The Early Days 119

Pa's Eyesight 121

Rosa 125

Rosa
An Italian Tale

BENVENUTI

My grandfather, Sebastiano Graziano, left the province of Naples, Italy at the age of nineteen to seek life and love in America.

He landed in turn-of-the century New York and set out to explore the country and seek his fortune. Traveling west to California and east again, he soaked up the cities and open spaces of this country. Having found work in each state of the union to support his travels, he decided that Chicago, Illinois was the best place for a working man to begin married life and raise a family.

My grandfather embraced America in a way that many immigrants did not. He learned English as quickly as he could and took classes at night to become an American citizen. But, more than that, he enthusiastically adopted the American spirit. Memories of my Grandfather evoke a broadminded and generous man who was deeply involved in the upbringing of his children. He supported the education of his son and daughters and remained a boisterous and jovial man even in the depths of the Great Depression.

My Grandmother, Rosalina Ambrosecchia, provided the quiet stillness that balanced the family. Born in the province of Avellino, she was an enchantingly beautiful woman. My Grandfather proposed marriage to her two weeks after they were introduced. With some trepidation, she accepted this brash young man's offer. Throughout their lives, he loved taking her on Sunday outings—much to the chagrin of the neighborhood ladies, whose husbands chose to spend Sunday afternoons away from home and family.

Much has been written about the immigrant experience and about how today's America has been shaped by the contributions of individuals not native to this country. These are the people who survived hardship, held their families together and chased the American dream. Their culture, humor, love and devotion not only provided the springboard for future generations, but also gave us the family values we all cherish.

I wanted to capture a sense of my family's life in Chicago during the first half of the twentieth century. Chicago was a dynamic place, full of growth and forward-thinking people. My family was a part of that dynamic.

This memoir is based on a series of interviews with my mother, Antoinette Ghilarducci, and her sister, Virginia Campobasso, who are now over eighty years old. The language and stories are theirs, unedited. I found their stories so enjoyable and so touching that I wanted to share them with readers outside of my immediate family. I hope you enjoy the liveliness and humor of these two women as much as I have. Welcome to my family.

THE GRAZIANO SISTERS

I'm Antoinette—I'm her mother.

Introduce yourself.

I'm Ant. I'm your MOTHER. I'm her mother.

Your name?

Antoinette.

Last name?

Ghilarducci.

And you are——?

I'm Eileen's aunt, her mother's sister, and my name is Virginia Campobasso.

Our maiden name was Graziano.

Where did you live?

***

Antoinette at their home on Grand Avenue.

HOME

(VIRGINIA "VEE"): I can only remember 1203 West Grand Avenue, a big, beautiful apartment building. About 10 apartments, all Italians. We lived on the third floor—4 rooms, a little bathroom. We hung clothes up in the attic. We used to take turns with other tenants. We carried clothes upstairs.

(ANTOINETTE): I can remember 627 Racine Avenue.

(VEE): That's where I was born.

(ANTOINETTE): I can remember my father carrying me up the stairs to look at the apartment that we were going to rent. I was in his arms, so I must have been 2 or 3 years old. But I can remember that!

And we lived there until they were making Ogden Avenue. So they had to tear down the building. So then we moved to 1201/1203. The drug store, Allegretti Drugstore, was 1201 and a dry goods store was 1203, on Grand Avenue.

Grand and Racine.

***

Rosalina and Sebastiano at 1225 W. Grand Avenue.

GRAMMA AND GRAMPA

Gramma came over from Italy?

(VEE): And Grampa was already here. Ambrosecchia—Gramma's maiden name.

Shortened to Ambrose. She was born in the province of Avellino Italy. And Pa was born in a province of Naples.

(ANTOINETTE): He came here first.

When he came to America he landed in New York and he was staying with his sister, I think. And he traveled by himself from New York, working his way across the United States in every state until he got to California.

From California he worked all the way back to New York and he found that of all the places that he worked in, he realized that Chicago was the only city for a working man to live in because it had a variety of industries. *How old was he then?*

He was I would say 19.

Where did he learn English?

He went to night school. But when he was that young he must have learned English along the way. When he was in Chicago he went to citizenship classes to become an American citizen.

Sebastiano

(VEE): He came here first and was living in Pittston, Pennsylvania. So he decided he wanted to get married.

And he was acquainted with my uncle, my mother's brother, Vincenzo Ambrosecchia. Now Grampa knew one other woman there, then. But he figured, no, she was too bossy.

And when my father wanted to find a "nice Italian girl"—my mother was a *beautiful* woman—he was introduced to my mother.

(ANTOINETTE): When he wanted to marry Gramma—what happened—my father only met her—2 weeks and he wanted to get married. He heard of her. My uncle's sister came from Italy and he wanted to meet her.

And when he said he wanted to get married in 2 weeks, Gramma said "No," she said to her sister-in-law, "I want to get to know him better." And her sister-in-law said, "My dear sister, you could know a man for 50 years, you will *never* know his habits or flaws. All I can guarantee to you is that if you marry my brother, you will never go hungry."

And sure enough.

(VEE): Gramma was—and my mother was *very* quiet, very quiet. But she was smart. Then she had to leave her brother because my father didn't want to stay in Pittston, a coal mining town. He didn't want to stay there.

My Grandmother's Italian Passport.
She arrived in New York in 1911.

"I have intentions of moving and going to Chicago," he said. So my mother had to leave her brother and come here to Chicago (thank *God*!). (*Laughter*).

She was an orphan?

(ANTOINETTE): Yes, yes. Her mother passed away first, when she was 7 years old. And she had 2 brothers. Then when she was 11 years old, her father passed away, but she was raised by an aunt and uncle.

Did she talk about Italy?

She would mention it.

She mentioned when she came to Pennsylvania she was so used to the fresh air and everything in Italy that she would go out and walk in the woods so that she'd get fresh air. But she adjusted. She adjusted.

***

Rosalina, at a wedding, 1942.

GRAMMA SILENT, BUT "FURBA"

(ANTOINETTE): My mother could not read or write in Italian or English. She never had schooling. She was a woman of very few words. But she'd come right to the point when she would tell you something. And you couldn't fool her with money. She knew her numbers.

She'd go shopping—she knew the right change. She didn't have schooling, but she was smart. It's a good thing she didn't have an education otherwise we wouldn't have been able to get away with *anything*!

(VEE): My father would talk talk talk talk, and my mother was quiet.

(ANTOINETTE): So one time she gets on the street car with my brother. They used to have a conductor and motor man. The conductor would collect the money.

Gramma was just looking at him and I guess she was a little slow in paying him. So the conductor says, he said to her, "Whad'ya looking at?!" She says, in English, "I looka you because you-a so-a good-looking." That shut him up.

* * *

THE STORYTELLER

(VEE): Grampa used to tell lots of stories. He was a storyteller. He spoke very good English.

(ANTOINETTE): He used to do skits. At women's clubs, settlement houses, the Chicago Commons. And he wanted to be an actor.

So there was this one time that he did this one skit about "Rosa." And every time he would tell me the story about Rosa, that he would practice, I would be *crying and crying.*

He used to go to different clubs. One woman—he got a letter. And she said can you please send me the story of Rosa. She wanted a copy of the story because it touched her so.

He would give different skits. Then he was going to a woman. He brought me with him. And this woman was giving him elocution lessons. But then, he gave it up.

He told stories in broken English. He spoke with an accent, but good English. He was a very smart man. He used to go to court and listen to the cases. And come home and tell us stories. He used to work nights and during the day he'd go to court and he'd listen to all these cases.

And what did Gramma think of this? She thought he was crazy.

***

"L'AMERICANO"

(VEE): And all the Italian men, they used to sit outside or stand on the corner in the old neighborhood and talk about Italy and this and that.

And Pa wouldn't hang around with them because he wanted to speak English. And they used to say "Oh the show off"—the "American"—over there.

(ANTOINETTE): And when he was taking citizenship classes they laughed at him. They said, what do you want to go and take citizenship classes for? We're working. We work. We don't have to learn English. We don't have to.

BUT when World War II broke out and they - the aliens - had to register, THEN they were scampering around. They got excited. They were worried that they would be shipped back to Italy.

So my father, he was the only man on Grand Avenue that became a citizen. "There's the American." He would never ever mingle in with the Italian men. No. Never mingled in.

(VEE): He used to take my mother downtown to the shows, restaurants, Thompson's Restaurant. Every Sunday my mother and father would go to Lincoln Park, to Navy Pier, Riverview. Sometimes with us.

And the Italian women when my mother would tell them, "Yesterday my husband took me and my daughter to Riverview," they were—ugh – their husbands took them *nowhere!* They would just go to church, the women, go to church, go home, put the apron on, and start cooking in the house.

And my father, after we had our *macaroni* dinner [*laughter*] every Sunday, then we would do the dishes and we would take the streetcar and go to the Navy Pier—walk on the boardwalk or just sit by the water.

My father would buy me ice cream cones. And walk. Go to Lincoln Park, to the zoo. And my mother would come home and say we went to the zoo, and the women would just *envy* her. My father was an American—he Americanized.

My father—we had the best of everything.

***

HOME LUXURIES

Your house didn't have heat?
(VEE): Coal.
You didn't have a refrigerator?
Ice box, ice box. The poor ice man.

By the time he came up to the third floor, he looked like an ice cube! Of course it was 25 pounds, a 25 pound weight. You'd put your sign on the window and when the ice man came, he would look up at the signs. And he'd see 25—or 50 pounds.

And with that big ice pick he'd pick it up. He had that big leather like a rug, draped over his shoulder. He'd put the ice on there, climbed up to the third floor, put it in the icebox. And sometimes it'd be like a little ice cube.

We had a pan under where the ice would melt. And every day we had to empty out the water. Sometimes we'd forget and we'd wake up in the morning and you'd find all the water and my mother would *holler* at us. The "ice-a box."

And you know what? We—the Italian people—still call the refrigerator the icebox.

And we'd put stuff outside in wintertime. The oranges came in a wooden box, and they'd nail it outside. My mother would put an oil—tablecloth—when it was worn out. And my father would cover the box so the snow and rain wouldn't go through the cracks. My mother put milk out there, meat.

We didn't use the icebox in winter, because the house was cold . You didn't buy milk in the store. You used to have a milkman. And we put the empty bottles outside.

The milkman, the coal man, the ice-a man, the beer man, the coffee man. Every Saturday. Those were the good old days, ohhhh.

***

GRAMMA'S JOB AND "LO SCIOPERO"

So did she work in Chicago?

(ANTOINETTE): Yes, she worked. Then, they used to work where they worked at home. She sewed trousers for tailor shops, and then she'd bring them back and get paid.

Then she worked in the nut factory, on Grand Avenue, by Sholti. We were grown up then. A nut-shelling factory. She went to the factory. First they brought the nuts home.

(VEE): We *ate* them *all!*

(ANTOINETTE): Later, it was against the law. You couldn't bring food for home work—jobs. So then she worked in the factory.

(VEE): And one time, they had a walk-out, a strike. All the women—all the *Italian* women—a sit-down strike.

And the children were coming home from school, expecting their mothers to come home and the mothers said, "We can't leave." Yelling out the window. "Tell your father to cook; I can't come home!"

There they were, all the Italian women, leaning out the window, with the white caps on their heads. A penny raise they wanted and they would not leave. Gramma couldn't leave!

(VEE) And all the husbands were coming home from work and "mama" wasn't home. "Where's your mother?" "She can't get out of the building." And the husbands, "Come down; come down; come home." But—they got the raise. A penny raise!

Ma came home and Pa didn't want her to go back.

***

The ladies at the picnic.
Rosalina is far right in both photos. 1937.

AT THE PICNIC

Who ARE these people? Okay—look at Gramma - how old is she?

(ANTOINETTE): I belonged to a club. This is Ma and this is Assunta and this is Florence's mother. So we decided that we would have a picnic and we would bring our mothers.

(VEE): Those women—look at THAT! They've got their legs up. The one picking Gramma up.

(ANTOINETTE): And they had a *ball*. They had a *good* time.

Earlier, Grampa had chased Uncle Joey out of the house and that day was the picnic and Ma didn't want to go. Pa said—you go to the picnic.

Then, Grampa used to pick on Joey. And Joey was never in trouble. There was something about Joe and Pa. When it came to my brother there was something. And my brother never was in trouble.

He had lost his job, and my father said, "You have to leave." So Ma didn't want to go to the picnic, and I said you've *got* to go.

This was 1937.

How old was gramma?

She was born in 1889.

So she must have been 48 years old in these pictures.

Rosalina gets a lift (left photo).

(VEE): All those women spoke Italian—Toscani—my mother was the only Neapolitan.

Wonderful reminiscing—can I come back?

***

Baby brother Joey, one year old, with sister
"Donette", age five, in 1919.

BABY BROTHER

You're the first born, then Uncle Joey and Auntie Vee.

(ANTOINETTE): Gramma didn't go the hospital—they had midwives.

In fact, when Uncle Joey was born, my father brought me to my godmother's house to stay there. When I went back the next day I had a baby brother whom I *adored*! I called him my sugarplum! I—AH—I just *loved* him.

Then when he grew up and he was like 2—3 years old, I had to watch him. I had to take care of him. Then he wouldn't let me out of his sight. Then I *hated* him because he just clung to me.

My mother could have gone out the door, he wouldn't say a word. As soon as I was near the door "D'onette, D'onette, D'onette." Ohhh!

***

BABY SISTER

(VEE): It was March 17.

The snow was 3 feet high and Gramma went into labor. And Grampa went to the doctor's, but he was out.

He didn't know what to do. And he went to Angelina la Barese and she came. He said, "My wife is in labor! My wife is in labor! We can't get the doctor."

So she left—she had about 11 children—and she ran over. And here my mother delivered me. I was already *born*! She said, "Oh my god! Santa Rosalina!" And she took care of me.

I never knew this. My mother never told us that. Everything about pregnancy was hush hush. They didn't discuss that.

So, when I got married this here woman was invited to my wedding. And when she came up to congratulate Uncle Johnny and me, you know, she says to me, "Do you know—does your husband know—that I was there when you were born?"

I said "Noooo, *I* didn't even know."

She says, "Yes," she said, "Your father was looking for the doctor and the doctor wasn't home and he came by me and I ran in the *snow* and you were already *born*. You were on the *bed*!"

At my wedding she's telling me this. My husband just looked at me. I said I didn't know.

So I told my mother, "You didn't tell me that Angelina la Barese" (you recognized people by what part of Italy they came from, where they came from. There was Angelina la Siciliana, Angelina la Barese, Angelina la Napolitana). I said, "Ma, you didn't tell me."

She said, "How did you know?"

I said "Angelina la Barese told me at my wedding."

"She had-a no business to tell you that."

Everything was hush hush. Every time it was my birthday my father would say "Whew".

It was on St. Patrick's day. Deep snow.

***

GENNY AND BENNY

(VEE): My father worked downtown at Marshall Fields, in the boiler room downstairs. My father. When he got through working, he would take the streetcar. And he would take State Street to Grand Avenue. Then Grand Avenue home.

So on Grand Avenue he would wait for the other streetcar. There was a peanut machine where'd you put a penny in there and you'd get a handful of peanuts.

Well, there were zillions of pigeons and when they'd see someone by the peanut machine, they'd flock over all around you. It was cold, he had an overcoat. Then they wore a coat down below their knees.

So, the streetcar was coming, my father put the penny in the machine, turned it, a handful of peanuts—threw those down, the pigeons gathered around him, so my father stooped down and grabbed two pigeons.

And he put one under each arm under the coat. And he got on the streetcar. From State and Grand, to Grand and Racine, those pigeons were under my father's ARMS.

And then when he came up the stairs he told my mother, "Here's two pigeons."

(ANTOINETTE): And are those the pigeons that Joey had as pets?

(VEE): Yeah.

So my father had made a coop up in the attic.

Up in the attic. We shared the attic with the other tenants. And we all had our own section to store things. So my father put the two pigeons in the coop. And we named them Genny and Benny.

(ANTOINETTE): And Joey, Uncle Joey—AHHHH—those were his pets. He would go up there for HOURS. He'd play with Genny and Benny in the coop.

(VEE): So one day my mother decides - they make the most delicious spaghetti sauce, flavor. They DO. So my mother—cooked—Genny and Benny. My brother didn't know.

(ANTOINETTE): So here we're sitting around the table eating our spaghetti and eating and all of a sudden he spotted it. He knew. He saw the pigeons.

"Are those—Genny and Benny?!"

My mother said "Yeah. We had to kill them. It was about time to kill them."

He cried, he cried, he cried—for Genny and Benny. And as he's crying, he's eating. "My pigeons! My pigeons!" And eating them. Eating Genny and Benny.

For years after we'd say "Remember Genny and Benny?"

* * *

Antoinette and Vee, on Grand Avenue. 1944.

LIFE WITH THE GRAZIANO SISTERS

(VEE): My mother used to go to Chicago Avenue. They were Polish people, Chicago Avenue and Ashland.

And {the} guy who came around in the wagon?

Peddlers would come with vegetables and fruit and they would have a horn. "Hey, PEEEEaches, Oranges, WaterMELON." And everybody would run downstairs with a purse and a basket.

The milkman, the iceman. Ma would go to the store though on Chicago Avenue, our shopping center. They sold things in bulk and she'd buy 5 pounds of graham crackers loose. And then she would buy candy chocolates, sometimes.

Sunday, we used to eat at 12 o' clock sharp. Pasta. By the time we did the dishes, my mother would dress us up and we would take a walk. Four blocks. To our godmother's.

Every Sunday we would go there. She had 8 children. We'd play in the back yard and our parents would visit. Every Sunday we would visit. We were so close. They were like cousin. Davvero.

(ANTOINETTE): I couldn't roller skate. Gramma wouldn't let me roller skate. She was so afraid I would hurt myself. So I was working. How old were you when I bought the roller skates?

(VEE): 10 years old.

(ANTOINETTE): I bought her roller skates, rented a

bicycle. She went horseback riding. My mother was working and [Vee] was doing the cooking when she came home from grammar school.

(VEE): I used to wash the house with cold water.

I used to meet Pa, I think it was State and Madison. No State and Monroe. I would take the streetcar and he would meet me after work, and he would take me to Thompson's Restaurant.

I had a girlfriend, Margaret, that I grew up with. And I would ask Pa if I could bring Margaret. She wasn't all Italian. Her mother was Irish but her father was Italian. And among the Italians she was called "La Polacca". Yeah.

Her and I were very good friends and she would come by the house and Gramma would say, "Margaret, eat, eat, mangia." My father and my mother liked her. So Margaret and I would go out.

And the other girls—Annie Lezzi, Luci Petromagli—they'd hear that we went to Thompson's Restaurant, and Margaret came with. It was like, "Wow." You know. I must have been about—was I in high school? I must have been in high school. He used to take us to restaurants.

You know, like I say, we were lucky that we could sit down and enjoy our parents. Especially our father. He told us stories. He was company to us. Whereas as all the other—comparing to all the other Italian fathers—all they did was get up, go to work, come home, eat. No association with their children.

My father was American. He was a family man.

***

THE WORKING MAN

(ANTOINETTE): First he worked for Marshall Field. No he worked for PF Paul [*garbled*] & Company. They're the company that made the Raggedy Anne dolls.

And then, at Marshall Fields, he worked downstairs in the boiler room. Like a janitor.

Then from there he worked in construction. He built the Oriental Theater, some other buildings. And then Depression set in. And during Depression, building just stopped. And then so after that, he went back to Marshall Field, and they hired him again. Immediately. Janitor work. Way down in the second basement, the sub-basement.

Sebastiano, on Grand Avenue

PA

(VEE): My father taught me all the Napoletana songs.

My father used to sing them. He would come home from work and he would shave, with the light bulb at the end of a chain. He would swing it over against the wall with the big mirror and my father would shave and sing at the same time. And I would sit on a chair next to my father, and I had that ear for music and I learned it.

I remember Grampa singing them, teaching me. I'd sit next to him and he'd say, "Repeat after me." We would sing together.

And he would teach me songs that had 4 verses to them. Like "Senza Mamma e' Innomorata" (without a mother). It was real sad, crying. I still remember all those songs.

The old songs, "Wey Marie", "Vicino Mare", "Mama". I knew the whole song "Mama." My father taught me. "Oh, MAMA" [singing]. My father sang all those Italian songs. "Santa Lucia."

I knew them all. I spoke Italian. I hung around with the Bareses and I knew how to speak Barese and Sicilian. And I spoke Neopolitan, because my father spoke the Neapolitan dialect more than my mother. Instead of "mangia," he'd say "mangna."

The girls with Pa, in back of apartment building
on Grand Avenue. 1930s.

When you were young—

(VEE): I would never talk. My father would say, "Say something." Instead, I'd say to Ma, "Io voglio pane", instead of asking my father. I was afraid to talk to Pa.

He would say, "Talk to me!" I never would. I'd say, "Ma—Ma." He said, "I'll give you a nickel. Talk to me."

Well! After a couple of years, I'd never stop talking. Then he said, "I had to give her a nickel to say hello, now I have to give her a dime to shut up!"

Our father spoke English to us.

When I was in high school all my homework had to be done with a typewriter—typed.

My mother wanted me home so I could wash the scarole, and get the supper ready. So I couldn't stay after school and do my homework on the typewriter. So I told my father.

He said, "Meet me at Marshall Fields," he says, "and we'll go shopping for a typewriter."

I still got the typewriter downstairs. And he bought me a typewriter. It's a Woodstock—$42.00. He paid $42.00. He took me to an office store where they sold adding machines, and everything. And he bought me a typewriter.

And I was the only one in class that had the typewriter. We carried it on the streetcar. [*Laughter.*] DING DING, DANG DANG.

Yeah, he was very very generous. Always gave us money to go to the show. And my girlfriend was included. Money for Margaret to go to the show. Like I said, I was close with my father. I was close to both of them. My mother, my father.

He was a smart man. My father was a very smart man.

He never owned a home. Never owned a home. Everybody saved to buy a house. A lot of them lost the house. But he never was one for painting. No, nothing. He was all thumbs to fix anything.

(ANTOINETTE): And my father took me to movies when I was real young. He was Americanized—until I was old enough to go by myself. He took me downtown to the shows.

He took me to see the play *ROSA*, a real play.

My father, he used to be hired for these different parties, to do his entertainment. I must have been 10 years old. And at these parties there were Americans. He went under the name "Tony Chico, Tony Chico".

Why did he pick that name?

(ANTOINETTE): Because Sebastiano Graziano - Tony Chico was better.

And one time he was on amateur hour on radio, Major Bowles. It was on radio and he did that skit "Rosa". It was an amateur show, on radio. And he won.

(VEE): And everyone was listening to the radio then. And he won a wristwatch. Elgin. And it was engraved, from the amateur show. Engraved.

And he gave it to me. Uncle Joe borrowed it and I never saw it again. He gambled it off. I said where's my wristwatch? And he said he gambled it off in a dice game.

Yeah, Tony Chico. Yes, he was smart. For not being educated. If he WAS educated he would have been something. Too bad he never went into business.

(ANTOINETTE): He played this part on the stage. There was an actor and his name was George Beban, the actor's name. Grampa learned the actor's part.

He would look in the mirror and act. "Sei Pazza— PAZZA!" Gramma used to say. Gramma.

THE HALLWAY

You always talked about the dark hallways—being afraid.
(ANTOINETTE): Oh yes.
The hallway was dark. They wouldn't have a light on.
We would have to go up one flight of stairs. The doctor's and dentist's office, and then the back part. And I was always worried that someone was lurking in the back and I'd RUN up the stairs, RUN down the hall—the long hallway .

And wasn't there someone named Mariucce who lived down the hall from you? You always talked about this lady named Mariucce....

***

MARIUCCE
(Mari-OOOCH')

Who's Mariucce?

(VEE): Awwwwww. Ohhhhhhh. Mariucce was our neighbor.

We lived at 1225 West Grand Ave. We had the third floor, front apartment. It was divided. Two apartments in the front and 2 in the back. Mariucce lived right by our back door, a hallway and her door.

And my ma and her became very good friends. And Mariucce she used to have a dog called Mikey. Mikey. She put a sweater on him. She treated it like a little boy.

Whenever she wanted something done in the house she would call me. She would call me, "VicinZELLA—VicinZELla" [*in a sing-song voice*]. "Vieni qua - vieni ca (dialect)".

And I would go and she'd say, "Get this for me, get that for me, do this for me." Anything.

When I come home from school, she knew the time. And her door would open, "VincinZELla." Go to the store and get me this and that. "OK Mariucce." And each time, I would always do that. And she would say, "When you get married, I'm going to get you a BEAUUUUUtiful present."

(VEE): She and my ma would sit in the back hall and talk and talk and talk. Very good friends. She would speak

Italian. *Was she from Naples?* She was from the region of Campania. And she spoke dialect.

Very good friends with my mother. And my mother was always so quiet. She wouldn't gossip about nobody. But we got all the news, all the gossip, from Mariucce. Maria.

Whenever she would have company—her "boarder", her "boarder". Well known. He would always come home with cases of fruit and he'd always say, "Hey, Mariucce, give some to Rosalina." That's my mother. "Give some to Rosalina."

So she would call, "Rosalina! Send Vicinzella. I'm-a gonna give you something."

Strawberries—CASES of them. I don't know where— who "gifted" them to him. He was like the syndicate. Okay, all right—is it all right that I say that? He was in the syndicate. He was the "DON."

He was really a don?

But he was the director of a funeral parlor. Shall I say the name of the parlor, Ant? No? Okay, I won't say the name.

(VEE): And he'd always bring cakes, sweets, Italian pastries, a dozen cannolis and whenever he'd bring them to Mariucce, he'd say, "Give some to Rosalina. Give some to Rosalina."

So she would call me, "VincinZELLA. Come over here." And I—I would just LOVE that and I'd say, "Ant, look, cannolis, strogatellis. All Italian pastries." What else? A lot of things we couldn't afford.

(ANTOINETTE): One time she called me over and she said, "Try these on." And they were kid gloves. She was very generous. I tried them on, they fit me. She said, "You can have them." He had brought them home.

(VEE): And when it was her turn to scrub the stairs. We used to take turns scrubbing the steps. Every Saturday the steps had to be scrubbed. One Saturday I would do it. The next Saturday, Mariucce's turn. *Well*, who would do it? ME! "Vicinzella, when you get married I'm gonna give you a BEEEAUtiful gift." In Italian she would say "Quando tu sposi, un bello regalo c'e date. Un BELlo regalo. VicinZELLA." I couldn't wait!

(VEE): So, when we got married, she was invited. She shows up. I couldn't *wait* to open up her envelope.

And, what does she give me? *Two dollars*! Hah. [*Laughter.*] But she was nice.

***

GIOVANNI

When did you start dating?
(VEE): With our husbands?
No, just dating.
Oh I always dated the "greaseballs." Because I spoke Italian they got a big kick out of it. All the other ones said a few words.

Then I used to go to the Paradise Ballroom dancing, with a girlfriend of mine from across the street. Her name was Connie Catalano.

And we used to go on Sunday afternoon. They used to have dancing at the Paradise Ballroom. On Pulaski and Madison? Ant? There was a beautiful ballroom and across the street was the Paradise Theatre.

This was in 1940. And they'd start dancing at 5 o'clock. We'd go dressed up in just a skirt and blouse, and carry our long gowns in a shopping bag with our shoes. On the streetcar.

We'd go to the dance hall, go into the bathroom. A lot of girls would do that. Their parents always thought they went to the movies. Then they used to have double features, so it would be about 4 or 5 hours. The dancing would go from about 5 to about 10 at the Paradise ballroom. There would be all the Italian boys in one corner.

So at the dance Johnny would always ask me, "Vee— dance?"

Dances were numbered then. And the eighth dance was a waltz.

"C'mon Vee—dance?"

It was the longest dance. Not that I want to brag, but Uncle Johnny was a TERRIFIC dancer. He was. So I—so that's all. He would walk me back and say thank you and he would always go dancing with other girls.

***

THE DON AND GIOVANNI

(VEE): So one Sunday I'm waiting on Grand and Ogden right in front of Michelletti's pastry shop. The streetcar, not the bus, the streetcar would stop there.

So Uncle Johnny happened to pass by and he sees me waiting there. And he says you going to the dance? I says yeah. He said, "C'mon in."

He was the only Italian boy in the neighborhood with a car. Because at one time he wanted to go back to Italy. He cried. He missed his mother, his brothers, his sisters. And he was here with his father.

So he wanted to go back because the American boys used to make fun of him. They used to tease him: "Hey, the greaseball!" And they used to teach him bad words. And he didn't know what he was saying. So he would say, "Pa, I want to go back." He said, "They're making fun of me."

So his father talked to "the Don" on Grand Avenue, the godfather. And he said my son wants to go back because the boys are chasing him.

The godfather said, "Give me their names, give me their names. And I'll put a stop to it." Because - EVERYONE—you BOWED when you saw the godfather! "Buon giorno, So and So, whatever his name was. Buon Giorno!"

So he talked to the godfather. He liked my father-in-law. Anyhow, he said, "My son wants to go back to Italy."

He said, "Listen, how old is he?"

"Nineteen. He wants to go back."

He says, "Mike, I can get him a car. How about that? That would keep him here."

My father-in-law says, "Well okay, let's try it."

So the "don" - he got one man to go get the car, with the rumble seat in the back. The back would open, and there would be a seat. A car. He'd get another man to get him a driver's license, and he would get somebody else to teach him how to drive.

So they would take Uncle Johnny to the South Water Street Market on Sundays. The market was closed and there was a wide street and this one fellow would take Uncle Johnny to teach him how to drive.

But somehow or other he had everything: a driver's license, and a car, everything, before he even knew how to drive!

Well, orders from "headquarters"—nobody—NOBODY—got in that car with Uncle Johnny unless the godfather told them who could go in.

And the godfather had a nephew and he said only he could go in the car with you. I don't want none of those boys that made fun of you in the car, otherwise I'll have the car taken away.

WELL, when Johnny was riding in the car, "Hey John, hey how are you?" THEN he had more friends than flies in the alley. But he couldn't take nobody in the car.

So he was the only Italian boy that had a car on Grand

Avenue. Johnny. Because the godfather knew he was a nice boy. A good boy.

So what did his father have to do to repay the debt?

Nothing.

No nothing. They lived in the same building. He was quiet.

***

Vee and Johnny.

THE COURTSHIP

(VEE): So one time, he said, "Get in the car." So we drove to the dancehall and we parked. I went to change into my gown with a big bow in the back of my head and my silver dancing shoes.

And they'd start to play the music and he danced with this girl and that girl. Then he would come and ask me. Instead of just the eighth dance, he'd ask me for the sixth dance, and the seventh dance, *and* the eighth dance.

And then he'd say would you like to go for ice cream. And we'd sit at the table. So he drove me home. I said thank you. The following Sunday, again, he picked me up and he said he would take me home.

So coming home he said, "Are you hungry?" You know me, I'm *always* hungry. So we stopped at a restaurant and he had a bowl of chili and I had a cup of coffee and a piece of cake and he drove me home.

And he said, next Saturday I'd like to go to the Lyons ballroom. Would you like to come there with me?

And I said, "Yes, okay."

And that was Saturday. He picked me up. Sunday we went to the Paradise Ballroom. So then he started to ask me to Navy Pier, on a Sunday before we went dancing. And we walked the pier.

When my mother met him, I think they fell in love.

She said, "Nice-a boy." He spoke Italian to my mother. And they'd talk about Italy, about the farm, and about the grapes, and this and that. And Gramma would say, "He's a nice-a boy."

And every Sunday he'd come and pick me up and say, "Does your mom want to come for a ride?"

So I'd say—"Ma, vieni per un giro a Navy Pier?"

She'd say, "Si, Si, va bene!"

We'd go to the pier, Lincoln Park. And they would talk and talk and talk. And there was a chemistry there. My mother just fell in love with him. He was a good boy.

I was about 18 years old. I was 20 when I got married. He was 7 years older than me. He thought I was older because I talked Italian and I was grown up. I wasn't silly.

Did you speak Italian together?

Yeah. Well I spoke Italian to him. And when we would go riding in the car, I would sing all these Italian songs that my father taught me. And I knew the Italian songs and Italian poems and Italian sayings.

He said, "You know all those songs? I don't even know those songs and you know them." "Oh Sole Mio." *Well*, when Uncle Johnny heard me singing those Italian songs I think he fell in love with me.

Then we got engaged. And I had a party at home with his uncles, aunts and cousins, the Nitti's. That was Valentine's Day. That December I got married. December 6.

***

Dolly and Antoinette, right, at 17 years old.

GRAND AVENUE
HUBBARD STREET

You grew up on Grand Avenue. And only a block away, there was Hubbard Street. But it was a "world" away.

(VEE): Oh, Hubbard Street was a "high class" block. All the....can I say the name? [*she asks Antoinette*] Yeah? All the "TOSCANI" lived there. And they thought they were so high class.

And on Racine and Grand Avenue they were mixed. Sicilian, Calabrese, Barese. But Hubbard Street, from Racine Avenue to Ogden, all Toscani. On one side, all the houses. And across the street was the viaduct.

They thought they were—you know—they used each word as if it was a $25.00 word.

(ANTOINETTE): The Toscani women were more modern. They cut their hair. The Toscani women. And the Italian women on Grand Avenue—their hair. Always in a bun. I don't know if the Toscani wore "mourning."

And on Grand Avenue, those women wouldn't *dream* of conversing with men. Like the neighbors, the men only—the men would be outside.

My mother, on left, with Gertie, visiting their
Hubbard St. friend, Dolly, on right. 1935.

(ANTOINETTE): The women never went outside. They'd look out the window. Out the window. The men would congregate. But on Hubbard Street, they would intermingle and the men and women would converse with each other. They were more broadminded.

I was in contact with Dolly. She and I were girlfriends. So at night I would go on Hubbard Street, instead of Grand Avenue. Not with the girls on Grand Avenue. I would go on Hubbard and would associate with her and her friends. And come home.

***

COVER GIRL

(ANTOINETTE): There used to be a man who would walk down the street, a neighbor. And everyone said he was an artist. And when he'd walk down the street he would look at me.

So years later, at the place I was working, they used to throw away old magazines. And one of my co-workers came up to me. This co-worker says Antoinette, you want to see your picture? And she showed me.

And I had a green dress like that. My girlfriend Dolly gave me this dress as a birthday present. And I parted my hair in the middle. And this girl was a neighbor and Vee, doesn't that look like Clare Carnevale?

(VEE): Yeah.

(ANTOINETTE): And Violet Saratella. And Me. And we used to have our drugstore. They used to serve drinks at the table. And you could sit down and have a sundae or a drink.

Now that's a coincidence! But I can't make out....it was 1935. But I remember him looking at me, every time.

Did you ever see him again after that?

No, but this [the magazine cover] was years later.

***

My mother, left, on the cover of Saturday Evening Post. September,
1935 issue.

Rosalina's Passport

"Ambrosecchia, Rosalina, daughter of Giuseppe…. Born July, 1889 in the province of Avellina."

Johnny and Vee at Antoinette's wedding 1945

Antoinette, 17 years old. Early 1930's.

July, 1932 postcards from Louie to Antoinette, then 17 years old.
Newspaper article from Chicago paper, August 9.

LOUIS

Who was the boy—you were really close to? When you were young. Was it Louis?

(ANTOINETTE): Louis.

Do you know you still have postcards from him? Here are 2 of them. Are those from him? Cause I was going through the pictures.

(VEE): Louis and her were only about 2 weeks apart. He went on vacation.

And then you kept the article too from the newspaper.

(ANTOINETTE): Ohhh. I didn't know that.

Who was he?

(ANTOINETTE): He was the oldest son of my godmother and we grew up together. *A Davvero?* Rosie's brother. Louis was the first born, then Rosie then Mary.

And we were close. We were like brother and sister. In fact, my godmother said when my mother used to go visit her, and bring me on Sunday, they'd put both of us in the same buggy and wheel the buggy.

He was 17 years old.

Here it says 20.

There was a car accident.

(VEE): Oh was that a waste!

(ANTOINETTE): He had gone on this vacation. His father insisted that he couldn't stay long, that he come home. So he came home early from the vacation. He and this girl, they were in the rumble seat. And that's when he got killed.

You said you were depressed.

Ohhhh, I dreamed about him for ten years. I dreamed, Louie, where were you? For *ten* years I dreamed about him.

But do you know, I dreamed about him, but I don't dream about Daddy. I only dreamed about Kathleen once, and that was her Mass and that Saturday morning was her Mass. I dreamed she came to my bed and she said, "Ma, Ma". And I woke up and I made the Mass in about 15 minutes. And that was the last time I dreamed about Kathleen.

I don't dream about my mother. But Louie, I dreamt about him for ten years.

I didn't know I had those postcards.

***

THE FEASTS

You used to talk about the Italian Feasts.

(VEE): On Grand Avenue, Hubbard Street. And up on Ohio street, right in front of the church.

The street was closed and they would have a procession on a Sunday with the statue and the ribbons. The statue— and it's HEAVY. There would be like 4 men on one side, with a big pole, and 4 men on the other side. And they'd walk with this crucifix.

And one man would be next to the statue with this wide ribbon, and as you donate money for a favor granted they would pin the money on the ribbon, and they'd yell [*in a sing-song voice*], "CINQUE PESA PER SANTA ROCCA FROM THE CAMPOBASSO'S!" and the band would go "badaboom badaboom badaboom."

Then they would shoot fireworks! Then the procession would continue.

And it took forever to get down one block -- because everybody wanted a favor granted by this famous saint. Either it was Saint Rocco, or a Barese saint, Sicilian saints. All these saints.

(ANTOINETTE): And they would have the man pushing his cart selling pumpkin seeds, cecci beans, booths everywhere selling lemonade, watermelon, sausage sandwiches. Fireworks.

One truck would be next to an alley and this truck would sell watermelon by the piece. And you could smell the watermelon because they'd throw all the rinds. All the rinds would be in a barrel. To this day when I eat watermelon, every time I smell a watermelon, to this day it reminds me of the feast.

Then they had the bandstand and they had a band. About a 50-piece band. And they would play opera. The people would stand around, and they had the wheel, and I had to be with Grampa and Gramma, you know, and they'd play this music. And the people would APPLAUD, right out in the street. They'd play a couple of operas. Opera songs, Neapolitan songs.

OHHHH, those Feasts!

And we'd have all our new shoes on and our feet would be killing us [*laughter*].

And everybody looking out the window. Nobody would want to leave their houses. And they'd be looking out the windows. Fireworks. Saturday and Sunday they'd have the fireworks. Women went too, families. People from all OVER. They'd be devoted to the one saint.

(And the girls, boys, oh YEAH,—all those ITALIAN boys—oooh.

Yeaaah—they still have it. Don't they have it? Ant?

(ANTOINETTE): They had the angels from one building to the other, at the feast of the crucifix. And they would have the angels come right over the crowds. They would have a 4th floor building on this side of the street and a 4th floor building on that side of the street.

Then they would put like a pulley line. And they'd have 2 little girls, 2 girls, dressed like angels, with a hook, and hook them on this here rope.

(VEE): Then they would lower them until they'd meet in the center and the people—in the street—on the sidewalk—they would recite in Italian, "SILENZIO, SILENZIO. Dio, Dio," a prayer.

And then after they'd say their part, the band would play and there would be fireworks, people would applaud and the old ladies would be crying, they had tears in their eyes. They had a prayer. The crucifix feast.

(ANTOINETTE): So one time, the Capodannos, a family, the Capodannos. They had 9 children. So the older girl and I, we were about the same age. And there was a younger sister, I forget her name.

We decided to "play" feast, so we hooked up this here younger sister to the clothesline, in the backyard. We almost killed her. She went BOOM. Right on the ground.

***

THE BLACK HAND

(VEE): The "Black Hand." That's how it started.

How old were you?

I think I was about 10 years old.

They would send a letter to those that had money and say you had to give us so much money and there was a print of a black hand on the letter, threatening them.

The Black Hand were definitely Italian. They demanded money and if you didn't pay them, people that were in business—grocery store, florist, pastry shop—you had to pay.

They'd demand so much because they knew you were making money in the business and you had to pay, to send them money. And if you didn't, they would break your windows, they would start a fire, throw a bomb.

You know the expression, "You'd better watch out or I'll throw a bomb in your house." It was an old expression.

They would destroy your property. They wouldn't harm the family. They wouldn't kidnap.

But one grocery store that I lived above, you could hear—then, the windows were bigger—you'd hear that break in the middle of the night, if you didn't pay up.

A lot of stores and businesses were boarded up. They weren't making enough money to pay protection. But they didn't bodily harm you. They would destroy your property.

But then when the syndicate come into power they wiped out the Black Hand. The syndicate was into other things, higher scale. They didn't bother the little business person.

***

EDUCATION

You didn't finish high school?

(ANTOINETTE): *Nooooo.* I was foolish. Very foolish.

Did you get sick of school?

(ANTOINETTE): Dolly's father passed away when she was 16. And she quit school because her mother wanted her home for some reason. And she got a job on the corner from where we lived, on Grand Avenue, and she was telling me all the fun they were having at work, all the fun. So I quit school and went to work.

What did grampa say?

He didn't like the idea. So then the place shut down and there I was. So Grampa said, "You have to go to school." So he registered me in a business college and paid for it.

(VEE): She typed.

(ANTOINETTE): Then we had to go to the Merchandise Mart building to register for jobs. That was major Depression, and I couldn't get a job.

Antoinette with girlfriend Celia - captured by a "cameo"
street photographer in downtown Chicago.
Late 30's early 40's.

So this Lina, she was working at the Bismarck hotel in the laundry and so she got me a job there. Folding sheets. Turning the sheets when they came out. And I worked there for about 8 years, something like that.

I hated it. I had a forelady, I hated her. I just hated her. So it got to a point where she did something, she started up the machine. We couldn't keep up.

So Caramella and I—I said, "For 2 cents I'd walk out". She said, "Well I can't take this heat anymore", because it would be hot you know. So we walked out.

And when I went home and my father came home, I told him I walked out from work.

What did Grampa say?

He gave me $10. He was generous.

***

Antoinette poses in front of a neighbor's car, early 40's.

CAREER PATH

(ANTOINETTE): We went on welfare.

A woman came over to the house to talk to Pa. But then she asked me if I could type and when I said yes, she said it would be better for me to get a job because it would pay more.

(VEE): Relief. We went on Relief.

(ANTOINETTE): So then I got a job at Tuckpoint and then I got laid off. I worked there and got laid off from there.

Then Adeline was working at Simpson Optical. This was still Depression, but they weren't doing war work. It was called civil defense, or preparing. So Simpson Optical used to make lenses for doctors. Then they went into war work, but it wasn't the war. And so I got a job there. And I started at $1.00 an hour.

(VEE): That was a lot of money.

(ANTOINETTE): And then when the war broke out they immediately changed over. I was making good money. I was working overtime. I worked there until I got married.

***

Antoinette poses by apartment on Grand Avenue.
Late 30's, early 40's.

WOMEN'S LIB

(ANTOINETTE): So this one time, I was working with this guy. He was making more money than I was and I was his supervisor. I saw his paycheck and he was making like 50 cents more than I was.

So I went into the office and I said, "I'm gonna leave." And the foreman said, "No, Antoinette."

Then I said, "I want to be a regular worker. Why should I have the responsibility of teaching somebody and *he's* getting more money than I am?" I said, you know, when my mother goes to the grocery store, they don't charge her less because her daughter's working and not making as much money as a man.

But the foreman told me, "No Antoinette, I have ambitions for you."

So did you stay?

I couldn't leave. I was making good money. I was working overtime. I saved my overtime money. I didn't hand it in at home.

***

BROOKS
...aka "Bruno Giovanni Vincenzo Ghilarducci"

Your turn. How did you even first know about daddy?

(ANTOINETTE): He was a second cousin of Dolly. Dolly was my friend. They had the same name—Dolly was a Ghilarducci.

He was 12 years old then, when I first saw him. And I used to say to her, "When your cousin Bruno grows up he's going to be good-looking." Because he was, he was a nice-looking little boy.

Then as he grew up [and] I vaguely remember that the few times that I would see him he always asked me to dance.

So one time I was dancing with him and Auntie Vee was at the same dance. And he was dancing with me and he was talking like he wanted to know me better. And I kind of shut him off. Oh, I knew that he was younger than I was.

So she said to me the day after, "Who was that boy you were dancing with at Eckert Park?" And I said, "Oh, that's Dolly's cousin. He wants to go out with me." She said, "Ant!!! What's wrong?" "He's younger than I am."

After that one time, Rosie, Celia and I, we happened to be walking, and he passed by with his car. And he took us for a ride. We went down to the Pier—Boardwalk [*laughter*] and went back. He took my phone number. But he never called me up.

Then I felt, well, you know. that's a lot of nerve.

So 3 or 4 months later, maybe a year later, I happened to be going to Celia's house and he had something to do with his club. So I said, "I'm going to my girlfriend's house," and he said, "I'll meet you."

So he met me on Grand Avenue. There was an ice cream parlor. He invited me to go to the ice cream parlor. And he had water and I had an ice cream sundae. Later on he told me he didn't have any money. He was so glad I ordered just a plain sundae because if I had ordered a banana split he wouldn't have been able to pay for it.

So at his sister's house—they were all going to meet. So he invited me to go. I knew his sisters. They were Dolly's cousins. They were kind of happy that he took me out.

Then after that, we were dating, and they were happy about that because they didn't like his friends, and they thought I was a good influence. So we went out. A few times. And then after that he never called me again. So he never called me. And that was it. I felt kind of—kinda hurt.

Then one day, around Christmas, I was writing a card and I said to Celia, I should send him a Christmas card. So she said, okay. She got me the Christmas card and she gave me the stamp and she said, go ahead send him the Christmas card.

So I wrote, "I hope you have a very Merry Christmas." And that was it.

So when he got the card, Christmas day, Lillian (his niece) came over. She knocked on the door, she came in. And she said, "My Uncle Brooks sent you this box of candy."

That was it. That was Christmas.

***

My father, Brooks, in the Army. 1941.

OFF TO WAR

(ANTOINETTE): Then it was in summertime. I was working. I used to cash my check on Chicago Avenue. There was a currency exchange and I used to cash my check there.

I cashed my check and then I'm walking down Noble Street to go home, and then I'd go down Grand Avenue. So on Noble Street, remember the Noble Inn tavern? So as I'm walking down, he comes out of the tavern, and he says he's going to drive me home—a block away—down Grand Avenue to Ogden Avenue. Just a block!

He told me that he got his draft papers. He was being drafted.

As I'm getting out of the car—Grand Avenue was very noisy—I said, "Goodbye, thank you." And he's talking to me. Normally I would say, "Yeah yeah". Something made me turn around and I said "What?"

And he said, "Can I call you up?"

So he remembered the phone number and I said sure.

Some of the photos Antoinette sent to Brooks during his
4 years in service....to make sure he wouldn't forget her.

(ANTOINETTE): The following weekend, it was on a Friday, he called me.

He said, "My family's stopping over".

Do you remember the tavern on Ogden Avenue? George's?

"My family's going to meet there," because he was leaving the next day.

I said, "Sure".

So he picked me up [and] brought me. There was his whole family. So then when he drove me home he said, "I want to write to you.

"Because," he said, "when you're away you want letters from home."

So I gave him my address. And that was it. It was before Pearl Harbor—because he went in September, and in December there was Pearl Harbor.

He was gone 4 years?

He was in California when Pearl Harbor was bombed.

***

LUCKY IN LOVE

(ANTOINETTE): So then he wrote to me. And it used to be, his family always called me Toni, he introduced me as Toni. So on the letter it was "Dear Toni," and then, he'd sign it "Your friend." "Yours truly."

So he would write and I wrote. I wrote to him EVERY day. Every day. Because I was going to make *sure* he wasn't going to forget me. I sent him pictures. He sent a letter 3 times a year! But I wrote to him every day.

When they were overseas, we had what they called "V-mail". You could fold it, and it became an envelope. Because they saved on the shipping.

I had a typewriter, and I would type, so I could write quite a bit. So when the mail call came, he always got letters. He was the envy of his soldiers. He got all this mail. "Ghilarducci?" "Yeah."

So then I'd get this letter. First it was "Hello Toni." Then, it was "Dear Toni."

Then he sent this one letter, "You know when a fellow's away he thinks of the girl he left behind."

And I thought, "Gee". And I look at the bottom and see "Love "—Wow! Oh my gosh.

(ANTOINETTE): Then I get a letter one day, "I wonder that if a certain boy would ask a certain girl…"

Daddy said that??

Oh he was very poetic, romantic—"if he would ask her to marry him, I wonder what she would say." Wow! I was, like, whew! I said, "I'm sure she would say yes."

So then he come back. I thought well, if he didn't ask me to marry him, that was it. I wasted enough time. It was 4 years later. That was it.

So when he walked me home he said, "Will you marry me?"

I said yes.

And then I said, get a job.

***

ASKING FOR HER HAND

Did he ask for your hand?

(ANTOINETTE): I said, "You have to ask my father." I said, "You have to ask my parents." So he came over. And my father came home late and he was eating at the table.

He said, "Mr. Graziano, I want your permission to marry your daughter."

So my father said to him, "Well," he said, he approved of him. "I'm honored that you asked me for my daughter's hand. But I have to tell you something about her."

Brooks thought, oh my god. He didn't know *what* my father was going to say. And my father said, "My daughter is a fine girl, but she can't get up in the morning."

And I thought, whew! Because Daddy couldn't get up in the morning.

So years later when we had the store and I couldn't come down early, he said, "I should have listened to your father!"

(VEE): The first time I saw Brooks he came to the house at 1225. They were going out and I had my tonsils out, and I was sitting by the oil stove. We had an oil stove.

It was cold, and he came in the door, the dining room. He said, "You should eat a lot of ice cream."

First time I saw him. I couldn't talk. ME—I couldn't talk.

***

Young newlywed Vee, 20 years old, with her Giovanni.
December 6, 1942.

WEDDING "LA SPOSA"

(VEE): In those days they were called peanut weddings. There were no sit-down dinners. Roast beef sandwiches were passed around.

Some friends would order the beef, order the bread, and then someone would go in the kitchen of the hall and they would make sandwiches, put them on a big tray, and pass them around.

People weren't sitting at tables. They were just sitting all around the hall. And that was called a peanut wedding. That was when I got married. They had beer, soda pop and wine. That was my wedding.

I got married in 19....when did I get married? 1942. December 6, 1942. A long time ago. December 6, during the war. That was called a peanut wedding.

We used to rent a hall and it was a Polish hall on Noble Street, near Ohio, was a hall. You had to bring your own tablecloth, clean the place up. And they'd come with a barrel of beer. Everyone would help serve.

Joey joined the Marines and would marry his sweetheart, Marie.
Antoinette is far left with hat.

When I got married, I had an apartment on—14 something Grand Avenue, and we had 3 rooms: kitchen, parlor, and a bedroom. And we had to share a bathroom. We lived in the front. We had to share the bathroom with the apartment in the back and we had a coal stove. December 6.

Before we got married, Johnny put coal in the stove. When we went to the apartment after the wedding, the stove died out. When we got back to the apartment, we were FREEZING.

So he had to shake the ashes, start the fire all over again. And we stayed around the stove. It was December 6—it was cold.

***

November 17, 1945

THE HAPPIEST DAY OF MY LIFE

(ANTOINETTE): My wedding was 1945, November 17.

And first there was a sit-down dinner at the Como Inn, Milwaukee Avenue. A sit-down dinner for about 60 people. Then not everybody was invited to the dinner.

And then, after, there were other people invited for just drinks and pastries and wine. Oh, there was liquor at my wedding.

How could you afford that wedding?

Daddy had come home from service with all [this] money. And he paid for everything. He wanted to pay for my dress too. I said, "No, I'll pay for that."

And where did you go for your honeymoon?

When we went to the hotel where we had a reservation, because it was after midnight, the reservation was cancelled. It was, this is like a pretty nice place. So then Uncle John Curielli, he said, "C'mon".

BGA

Mr. and Mrs. Sebastiano Graziano
request the honor of your presence
at the marriage ceremony of their daughter

Antoinette

to

Mr. Bruno B. Ghilarducci

on Saturday afternoon, seventeenth of November
Nineteen hundred and forty-five
at three o'clock

Santa Maria Addolorata Church
corner May and Erie Streets
Chicago, Illinois

Reception eight o'clock at
Como Inn
546 Milwaukee Ave. cor. Ohio St.

From Antoinette's Wedding Album

Brooks' older sisters, Marge, left, (friend Yolanda),
Mary in middle, Yolanda and Jo.

So he took us to a place. It was clean and no one bothered us. It worked out better.

Didn't the bed break?

I just got up and I said, "I'm gonna go back to bed" and then BOOM - the whole thing caved in.

I said, "What are they going to think?" It was on Madison Street.

***

ITALIAN TRADITION

(VEE): By Italian tradition, usually they name the firstborn after the father's father, if it's a male. If it's a female, after the father's mother. So which I did. My father-in-law's name was Michele, and we called my son Michael.

By right, the second son when he was born, by right, according to the Italian tradition, you name it after the mother's father. Which would have been my father. But since his name was Sebastiano and in American it's Sebastian, I just couldn't picture myself naming the boy Sebastian.

So when I was pregnant with Jack [*her second son*], I said, "Pa, if this is a boy, I said, you wouldn't be mad if I don't name him after you?"

I would have named him after my husband, Johnny. So I had told Grampa that and he said his feelings aren't hurt.

"My feelings won't be hurt, if it's a boy and you don't name him after me; if you name it after your husband".

When I was, when WE were pregnant [Antoinette and Vee were pregnant at the same time] with Rosalyn, I asked your mother, "If you have a girl are you going to name her after ma?" She said no.

And I said, "Well, if I have a girl, I'm not going to name her Constantina", my mother-in-law's name, "because they call her Tina. There are 2 Tinas already." And I told Uncle

Johnny, I said, "John, if this is a girl, don't get mad if I don't name her after your mother".

And he looked at me and then I said, "If it's a girl, I want to name her after *my* mother". And he said, "Oh YES!" Oh he loved Gramma! He said, "YES—if it's a girl, YES." So it was a girl. So when Gramma came to the hospital, I said, "Ma, we named the baby after you—Rosalina."

"Oh no no no no," she goes. "You gotta name him for Johnny's mother, Johnny's mother." I said, "No, Johnny said it's okay, he wants us to name her after you: "Rosalyn" [Rosalina]".

And Gramma was *proud.* She had a soft spot, yeah, for Rosalyn, yeah, yeah. Gramma was happy. I said, "Johnny wants to name her after you too".

(ANTOINETTE): I wouldn't name it after anybody. I worked with this friend, we became very good friends, and her name was Eileen, and I thought that was such a pretty name. And Kathleen.

So when you were born, I said to daddy, "How about Eileen," because I worked with this girl and I thought that was so pretty. He said, "Yeah, that's okay." I didn't follow the tradition.

***

Rosalina and Johnny. Early 1940s.

TAKING SIDES

(VEE): When Uncle Johnny and I would disagree and we would argue, Gramma would just sit there, listen.

And I would say, "Ma, who's right, who's right? Aren't I right?"

She'd say, "You wrong-a and SHUT-A UP!" Shaddup!

YEAAAH, how about that, she didn't even stick up for her daughter. Oh yeah. He loved her.

***

Antoinette behind counter, Rosalina next right,
with customers. Circa 1947.

BROOKS GROCERY

How did you and Daddy decide to get the store and get into the business?

(ANTOINETTE): Well, when daddy came home from service he had a lot of money, and he always said he wanted to go into business. So first he's thinking of a tavern, and there was one on the corner. He was looking into it.

And then meanwhile we were living with his father, and there was this grocery store, not even a half a block from the house, that I used to go there.

Were you living on Hubbard Street then?

Yes. 1419, I think. So our house was further west, just west of the store, the next block over. And I went to the store.

There was a butcher and this little bit of a grocery store. They didn't sell much groceries. And the woman said they were selling. They were leaving and they were selling.

So I immediately went over and I said to Daddy, "You know, Brooks, they want to sell the store. And the house." And I said, "Go and find out how much she wants." So he went.

Later, she showed us the flat upstairs. There was a woman living there by herself and she asked if we could come in and look at it with the 4 rooms.

And so then we went downstairs and she said she wanted $6,000.

That was in 1947, 1948?

Yes. Just Kathleen was born. She was just a baby.

And so we thought we had just so much money and we thought maybe we could get a loan from the bank. Well, we couldn't get a loan from the bank.

Did you try?

Yes.

And meanwhile—were you working at the time or just Daddy?

Just daddy. He was working. Cause we had Kathleen.

So somehow or other we had this lawyer—that Uncle John knew—John Curielli. So he got the loan for us. He had connections that he could get the loan for us. So we got the loan. And got the store.

***

LEARNING THE TRADE

How did daddy learn about—you didn't have any background in meat.

All I said to him was, "This woman came over and said they're selling the store, they're moving".

So I said to Daddy, "Can you cut pork chops?"

He said, "Who do you think cut the meat when I was in the service?" [*He was a cook in the army.*]

But there, he'd go out, and shoot a sheep or something, and chop it up, and cook for a whole army.

So meanwhile we had this friend Jim LaForti, that worked at the market. And he knew about it. So he taught Daddy different things about how you cut the animals. And he brought him to the meat market, on Randolph Street, showed him how to buy the meat. And the produce.

And, at the store, sugar was still being rationed. And flour. And meanwhile, with the little bit of money we had, we went to the market and bought groceries, and daddy painted the store. And we got in touch with all the service men for the bread and the cakes and all that.

And meanwhile with our ration book I bought sugar whether I needed it or not. With the ration book. So we had like 6 5-pound bags of sugar. And Gramma had some, so we bought more from her book. So then Gramma come to live with us. Was she? Who was she living with? No not yet, she came after. After Pa died.

So we got her ration book for the sugar, and little by little, we bought. And as we sold stuff we bought more.

And then one of the grocers that we bought from, they let us buy and pay the following week. So when we sold it we paid. Little by little we started building up our stock.

And when they came in, the customers, they said, "Oh this store never had this much stock." So, we were kind of encouraged.

And then we moved into the back of the store, the back of the building. And then the lady was still living upstairs and paying the rent.

Meanwhile, when the store was closed by the original people, well, their customers went to Grand Avenue. And then where the Noble Inn is, it was almost like a supermarket.

But those customers came back to us. And they were passing by our store, looking in to see what gives.

So little by little.

***

Little Oscar visits Brooks Grocery.

THE STORE—THE EARLY DAYS

(VEE): That was a happy house then—I lived upstairs. I took care of Kathleen and Jack. We were all together.

(ANTOINETTE): When we bought the building, I figured, well, I had Kathleen. So we had Auntie Vee come from where she was living, or your dad used to bring Kathleen every morning. Little apartment, Grand Avenue. And she cried and she cried and she cried.

(VEE): And then you said the woman came to take her stuff out. "Vee the apartment in back, would you like to come and live upstairs?" And I said okay. So Uncle Johnny went and painted it and we lived upstairs. And I had Jackie, Mickey, and watched Kathleen.

(ANTOINETTE): You take care of Kathleen

(VEE): And she only charged me $10 a month rent.

(ANTOINETTE): We didn't want to charge her.

(VEE): I had gas, electric, water was on the meter in the store, because the people had upstairs and downstairs. So they had only 1 meter. I was paying $25 where I was living on the third floor. Lucky thing she didn't say "How much do you want to pay?" I'd say $30.

So she said $10 a month and you watch Kathleen. Johnny wanted to pay more.

And your father used to give me a big pork loin. "Vee, here. You cook and we all eat together. Neck bones, sausage and ground beef. "Here, you cook, and we eat together" (on Sunday). They had the store open on Sunday.

PA'S EYESIGHT

(ANTOINETTE): Grampa started losing his eyesight. Cataracts. Considered a serious condition then. He went for surgery. *Was he able to see?*

(VEE): You're not going to tell that story?

You told me that story before.

(ANTOINETTE): No, I didn't tell her. What did I tell you?

That he was so depressed about his eyesight.

(VEE): He couldn't see. He couldn't read no more. Then, it wasn't like today. Today you get your eyesight back right away. Then, it wasn't, and he thought he was blind, that he'd never be able to see. And he went into a state of depression.

We couldn't find him. We couldn't find him. So we reported it to the police. Maybe he got lost, he couldn't see.

Then we got the phone call. So Gramma didn't go down. Johnny and your Dad, they went.

You didn't go?

They wanted the men of the family.

"Send the men."

You were already married? (ANTOINETTE): I had Kathleen. (VEE): And I had Jack. That was in 1948, Labor Day. We were going to have a party for Kathleen that day, and your mom had to call all your aunts.

How did they find him? How did they know where to look?

(ANTOINETTE): Just floating, face-down. Just floating.

The Chicago river?

Yeah.

So we went to get Gramma. She sensed it, she sensed it. We told her. And Gramma never went back. To the house. She stayed with us. That's when she stayed. She stayed with me.

***

ROSA

(ANTOINETTE): Grampa used to do skits. So when he used to go out on these here parties where they would hire him, he would tell this here story about Rosa. And he'd take me with him, and I'd listen to it and I'd cry.

The story started out....

There was an Italian man and Rosa was his daughter. And he wanted—he didn't have any money—and he wanted to buy a Rose, for Rosa.

And, so he goes into the flower shop and he wanted to buy just one rose. And he said, "I would like to buy a rose."

She said—the woman that owned the shop said—that will be $5.00.

He said, "But I only want *one* rose."

So then there was a society woman in the shop. She was buying flowers and she was listening. She had a sheath of roses in her arms.

And he says, "You know," he says, "My little girl Rosa, when I would come home from work, she'd say, 'Pa PAAA'. And Rosa would RUN to me and hug me.

And one day I come home and I say, 'Rosa, Rosa.' And Rosa doesn't answer. My little Rosa died. That's why I want this one rose. To put on her grave, my little Rosa's grave," he said.

So this woman, the society woman, she hands him her bouquet of roses—for Rosa.

And that was the end.

This was a play?

And when she gives him the roses, the curtain comes down.

The End.

EILEEN GHILARDUCCI ARNOFF

To the memory of my immigrant grandparents, Sebastiano Graziano and Rosalina Ambrosecchia Graziano.

GRAZIE

Assembling the material was easy. I had the two best entertainers to tell me story after story. The hard part was maintaining the drive to finish the project.

To that end, I have special thanks to my motivators and those who inspired me: Pam Kinzie and Marilyn Errett. Neither is Italian, but they found this material so entertaining, it spurred me to keep moving and see this project through.

Gretchen De Limur, Beca Smith and Keri Nevil supplied technical knowledge and enthusiasm to push me along.

Of course, Antoinette, my mother, and Virginia, my Auntie Vee, provided all the entertaining stories. A salute to my cousin Jack Campobasso, who said, "Ask my mom to tell you the story about the pigeons."

And to Larry Arnoff. With him in my life, there was plenty of quiet encouragement every step of the way.

And special gratitude to my mother, an amazing woman.

Grazie tutti.

CHICAGO, THEN AND NOW

Marshall Fields, where my grandfather worked in downtown Chicago, still proudly displays its ornate clock on State Street.

The Oriental Theatre, that he helped build, has been restored and can be enjoyed by today's generations.

Navy Pier is a highly touted tourist attraction today, after having been renovated. The older Navy Pier had a homier feel, but the views along the lake still entice now as they did then.

The Bismarck Hotel was remodeled in the 1990s to a new, modern hotel.

Lincoln Park remains a lakefront recreational retreat for all to enjoy. And the zoo, yes, is still there.

No longer there, is Thompson's Restaurant, or the scene of Vee's courtship with Johnny, the Paradise Ballroom.

The South Water Street Market is gone, but the Randolph Street Meat Market sort of exists. The area has been gentrified with plenty of fine dining restaurants.

The Como Inn restaurant offered up fine dining and venues for weddings through the 1990s.

Riverview was Chicago's rough-and-tough Disneyland, and thrilled adults and children well into the 1960s. It was suddenly dismantled and remained a large empty parking lot for years (near Belmont and Western). Ask any old-timer Chicagoan, and they'll all lament that it was the greatest amusement park ever.

Hubbard Street and Grand Avenue are now an up-and-coming neighborhood just minutes from downtown Chicago. Most of the old homes have been replaced by brick high rises and townhomes.

The corner of Grand Avenue and Noble Street is where the Noble Inn stood. The building is still there, but not the tavern. At Ogden Avenue and Hubbard Street was the tavern where Brooks said goodbye to Antoinette.

The viaduct still runs along Hubbard Street near Racine Avenue where the Toscani people congregated. My mom and aunt's home on Racine and Grand, I am told, burned downed and has been replaced by a brick building. But 1225 W. Grand Avenue still stands.

Antoinette and Brooks toiled away, happily, at Brooks Grocery and Meat Market for close to 40 years. They sold the business in the early 1980s.

The grocery store, on Hubbard Street, is now a restaurant called "The Breakfast Club," serving up the best breakfasts in town. While the interior has been changed, the building still stands, one of the few originals left in a fast-changing neighborhood, with little remnants of its Italian past.

The subway will still take you from downtown Chicago to Grand and State Street (the beginning of Genny and Benny's demise), and the Grand Avenue bus will then deposit you at Grand and Racine Avenue. The streetcars, of course, are no longer running. And I haven't checked to see if the peanut machine remains.

AUTHOR'S NOTE

There was indeed a vaudeville piece in which George Beban starred for five years, called the "Sign of the Rose". A film version of the play opened in 1915 under the name "The Sign of the Rose, and also under the title, "The Alien".

In showings in theaters around the country, the film ended as the character Pietro enters the flower shop to buy a rose for his daughter's coffin. The curtain then rose and lights came up on a stage set of the flower shop.

The actors from the film then appeared live and enacted the denouement, which lasted for approximately thirty minutes. Actress Blanche Schwed played the role of the daughter, Rosina, or....Rosa.

***

AUTHOR'S BIO

A third generation Italian-American, Eileen Ghilarducci was raised in Chicago by "Americanized" parents. They encouraged her to study in Rome, and she also worked in Italy.

One of her greatest joys in life has been rediscovering her Italian roots through the stories of her mother, Antoinette, and her mother's vivacious younger sister, Auntie Vee. This exploration of her past ultimately inspired her to record and transcribe her family's stories. She currently lives in Napa Valley with her husband, where they tend to a small vineyard and savor the slow pleasures of life together. *Rosa, An Italian Tale,* is her first book.